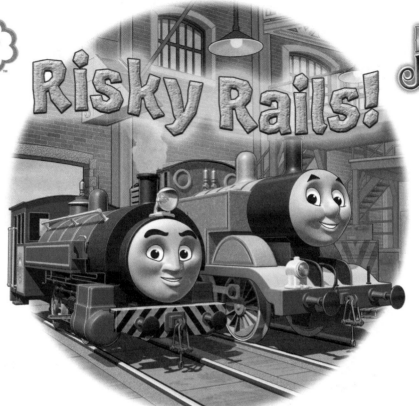

Illustrated by Tommy Stubbs

A Random House PICTUREBACK® Book

Random House 🏠 New York

Thomas the Tank Engine & Friends™

CREATED BY BRITT ALLCROFT

Based on The Railway Series by The Reverend W Awdry.

ISBN: 978-0-307-97674-1

randomhouse.com/kids   www.thomasandfriends.com

Printed in the United States of America   10 9 8 7 6 5 4

HIT entertainment

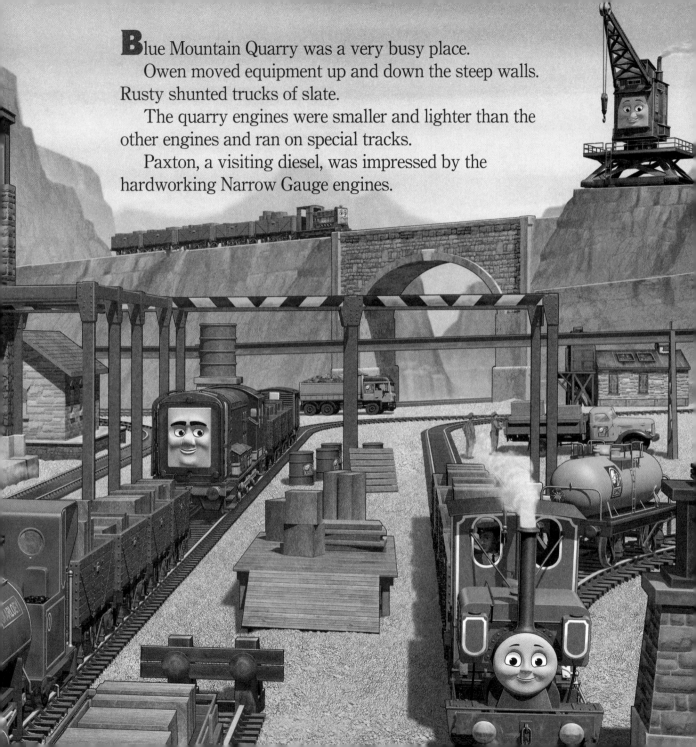

Blue Mountain Quarry was a very busy place.

Owen moved equipment up and down the steep walls. Rusty shunted trucks of slate.

The quarry engines were smaller and lighter than the other engines and ran on special tracks.

Paxton, a visiting diesel, was impressed by the hardworking Narrow Gauge engines.

Suddenly, with a rumble, Blondin Bridge began to collapse!
Rheneas saw the danger ahead and tried to stop. But his heavy
load pushed him across the bridge.

Rheneas was safe! Everyone
was relieved. Then they saw
poor Paxton, half buried in stone.
He wasn't hurt—but he needed
some repairs.

Sir Topham Hatt asked Thomas to work in Paxton's place.

"I like working with my Narrow Gauge friends," he peeped. He chugged off to the quarry, where he was met with whistles of welcome.

The work at the quarry was hard, but Thomas enjoyed it.
Suddenly, a small green engine darted out of a tunnel.
"Hello," Thomas peeped, but the engine rolled into another
tunnel without answering.

The next morning, Thomas saw the little green engine again. "Who are you?" Thomas asked.

The little engine puffed off without answering. Thomas tried to follow.

"Go, Luke!" Skarloey cried as he and the other Narrow Gauge engines blocked Thomas.

"Who is Luke?" Thomas asked Skarloey. "Why does he run away?"

"He hides because long ago he did something very bad," Skarloey said. "He's afraid that if he's found, he'll be sent away from Sodor forever."

Thomas promised to keep Luke's secret.

Later, Thomas steamed off alone to think. "Don't worry, Luke," he said aloud. "I'll find a way to help you."

Someone was watching. . . .

The next day, Luke emerged from a tunnel and approached Thomas. "I'm sorry I hid from you," he said. "Will you be my friend?"

"I'd like that," Thomas replied.

Thomas and Luke worked together at the boulder drop.

Thomas asked Luke why he had to hide. They didn't notice that Paxton, who had returned to the quarry, was listening as Luke told his story.

"I came to the Island of Sodor by boat," Luke began. "There was also a little yellow engine who spoke a strange language."

"While I was being lifted off the boat, I bumped the yellow engine, and he went splashing into the sea."

Paxton couldn't believe what he had heard. He raced
off to tell Diesel.

At that moment, an idea flew into Thomas' funnel. "I know
what I'll do!" he said. "I'll find out what happened to that little
yellow engine. Maybe he's at the Dieselworks!"

Thomas was shocked to hear Paxton repeating Luke's story to Diesel.
"We have to tell," said Diesel. "Luke will have to leave Sodor forever!"
Thomas had to find the little yellow engine. He chuffed to the
Steamworks to talk to Victor.
"That engine was *me*," Victor said.

Victor's story about his journey to Sodor matched Luke's. But there was one big difference. "The chains holding my wheels were broken," he said. "That's why I slid into the sea when the green engine bumped me."

"When Cranky fished me out, I was in a terrible state."

"It was an accident!" peeped Thomas. "And you were repaired!"

"Yes," said Victor. "I chose to be painted red—a new color for my bright new life!"

"I have to tell Luke!" Thomas said.

"Is Luke the little green engine?" asked Victor.

"Yes," said Thomas. "And he needs your help."

Later, Diesel and Paxton found Luke at the quarry. Luke rolled up the narrow-gauge tracks, where Thomas and the other engines couldn't follow.

"You can't hide now!" shouted Diesel. "Sir Topham Hatt is coming to kick you off Sodor! Even Thomas can't save you!"

"Yes I can," Thomas peeped as he sped into the quarry.

Rocky and Owen helped Thomas climb all the way up the quarry's walls.

But Thomas' wheels were too big for the narrow gauge tracks at the top. They jumped off the rails and Thomas rolled toward the edge of the cliff. "Help!" Thomas peeped. Just then, Luke came around the bend.

"Watch out, Thomas!" cried Diesel. "He's going to push you off! Just like he did to that yellow engine!"

"Don't worry," said Luke. "I'll pull you back to Owen." And slowly but surely, he pulled Thomas back toward the platform. Luke felt strong!

Luke got Thomas safely to Owen's platform, but the two engines weighed too much for Owen. The platform began to drop straight down!

"Cinders and ashes!" peeped Thomas.

Gears whined! Sparks flew! But Owen brought Thomas and Luke safely down.

Just then, Sir Topham Hatt arrived with Mr. Percival, the narrow gauge controller. They were confused and angry.

Then Victor steamed into the quarry.

"Luke, you didn't push me," he said. "It was an accident!"

Sir Topham Hatt was upset with Diesel. "You didn't find out what really happened," he said. "And the real story is what matters."

"Well done, Thomas," said Sir Topham Hatt. "Today is a happy day for Mr. Percival and his engines."

"Thomas has made it a happy day, Sir!" Luke said. "He's my hero—and my friend!"

Thomas and all his friends, new and old, whistled happily.